THE ILLUSTRATED COLLECTION

THE RED-HEADED LEAGUE

SCAN THE CODE TO HEAR THE STORY!

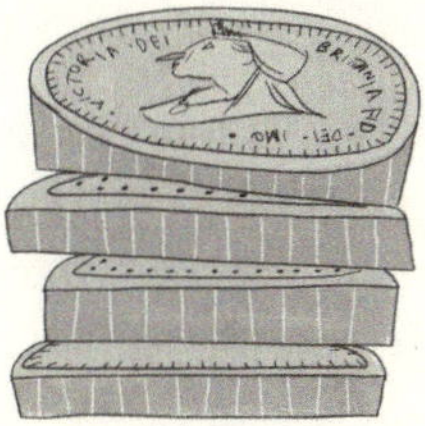

Chapter One

One day in autumn I called upon my friend Sherlock Holmes in our old rooms in Baker Street. Since my marriage, we had not seen much of each other. He was frequently engaged on some case, while I was busy establishing my own medical practice. Despite my happiness with Mary, I found that I missed the excitement of life with Holmes. Since the man often forgot to eat when investigating a problem, he certainly wouldn't remember to keep up with his acquaintances. The only way I would hear what he had been up to was if I were to pay him a visit.

On stepping into the study I had once shared with Holmes, I was surprised to see how neat and orderly it was. Mrs Hudson had clearly been looking after him; I could not imagine the detective thought it particularly important to keep his quarters clean.

I found him deep in conversation with a very stout,

elderly gentleman with fiery red hair. I apologised for my intrusion and was about to leave when Holmes pulled me into the room and closed the door.

'You could not possibly have come at a better time, my dear Watson,' he said warmly. He turned to the gentleman.

'Mr Wilson, may I introduce you to Doctor Watson? He has been my partner and helper in many of my most successful cases, and I have no doubt that he will be of the utmost use to me in yours also.'

The stout gentleman half rose from his chair and bobbed his head in greeting. He gave me a quick little questioning glance but seemed reassured by Holmes' introduction and resumed his seat.

I sat on the sofa and waited for whatever mystery this man had brought to Holmes to unfold.

Holmes put his fingertips together, as he often did when deep in thought. 'I know, my dear Watson, that you share my love of all those events outside the humdrum routine of everyday life. You have shown your delight in the bizarre by being so eager to write down, and to embellish, so many of my own little adventures.'

'Your cases have indeed been of the greatest interest to me,' I said sincerely.

'You will remember that I said the other day that life is often stranger than anything the imagination can conjure up.'

'And I doubted it.'

'You did, Doctor, but nonetheless, you must come round to my view, otherwise I shall keep piling facts upon you until you have to agree that I am right. Now, Mr Jabez Wilson here has been good enough to call upon me this morning, and to begin a story that promises to be one of the strangest that I have listened to for some time. You have heard me say that the strangest and most unique things are very often connected to the smaller crimes. Sometimes there is some doubt as to whether a crime has been committed at all.

'As far as I have heard, it is difficult to say whether the present case is a crime or not.

Perhaps, Mr Wilson, you would have the great kindness to begin your story again. I ask not only because my friend, Doctor Watson, has not heard it, but because it is so strange that I am anxious to have every detail repeated. I am usually able to guide myself by the thousands of other similar cases that come to mind, but the facts in the present instance seem to be unique.'

The portly client puffed out his chest proudly and pulled a dirty and wrinkled newspaper from the inside pocket of his greatcoat. As he glanced down at it, with his head thrust forward and the paper flattened upon his knee, I took a good look at the man, and tried, as Holmes would do, to understand Mr Wilson's character by considering his

appearance. I did not gain very much, however. Our visitor looked like an average British tradesman. He wore rather baggy grey check trousers, a not very clean black frock-coat, unbuttoned in the front, and a drab waistcoat with a chain and a square, pierced bit of metal dangling down as an ornament. A frayed top hat and a faded brown overcoat with a wrinkled velvet collar lay upon a chair beside him. Altogether, there was nothing remarkable about the man except for his blazing red hair and the expression of extreme irritation upon his face.

Holmes' quick eye saw what I was doing and he shook his head with a smile. 'Beyond the obvious facts that he has at some time done manual labour, that he is a Freemason, that he has been to China, and that he has done a considerable amount of writing lately, I can deduce nothing else.'

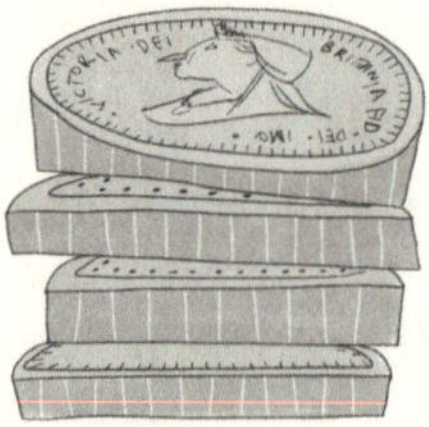

Chapter Two

Mr Jabez Wilson sat up in his chair with his forefinger upon the paper but his eyes upon my companion.

'How did you know that, Mr Holmes?' he asked. 'How did you know, for example, that I did manual labour? It's as true as gospel; I began as a ship's carpenter.'

'Your hands, my dear sir. Your right hand is almost a size larger than your left. You have worked with it, and the muscles are more developed.'

'Well, the Freemasonry?'

'Rather against the strict rules of your order, you wear an arc and compass breastpin.'

'Ah, of course, but the writing?'

'Your right cuff is very shiny for five inches and the left one has a small patch near the elbow where you rest it upon the desk.'

'Well, but China?'

'The fish that you have tattooed just above your right wrist could only have been done in China.

I have made a small study of tattoos and have written on the subject. That trick of staining the fish's scales in a delicate pink is peculiar to China. When, in addition, I see a Chinese coin hanging from your watch-chain, the matter becomes even simpler.'

Mr Jabez Wilson laughed. 'Well, I never,' said he. 'I thought at first you had done something clever, but I see that there was nothing in it after all.'

'I begin to think, Watson,' said Holmes with a frown, 'that I make a mistake in explaining. It will do little for my reputation. Can you not find the advertisement, Mr Wilson?'

'Yes, I have it now,' he answered, with his thick, red finger planted halfway down a column on one of the newspaper pages. 'Here it is. This is what began it all. You must read it for yourself, sir.'

I took the paper from him and began to read.

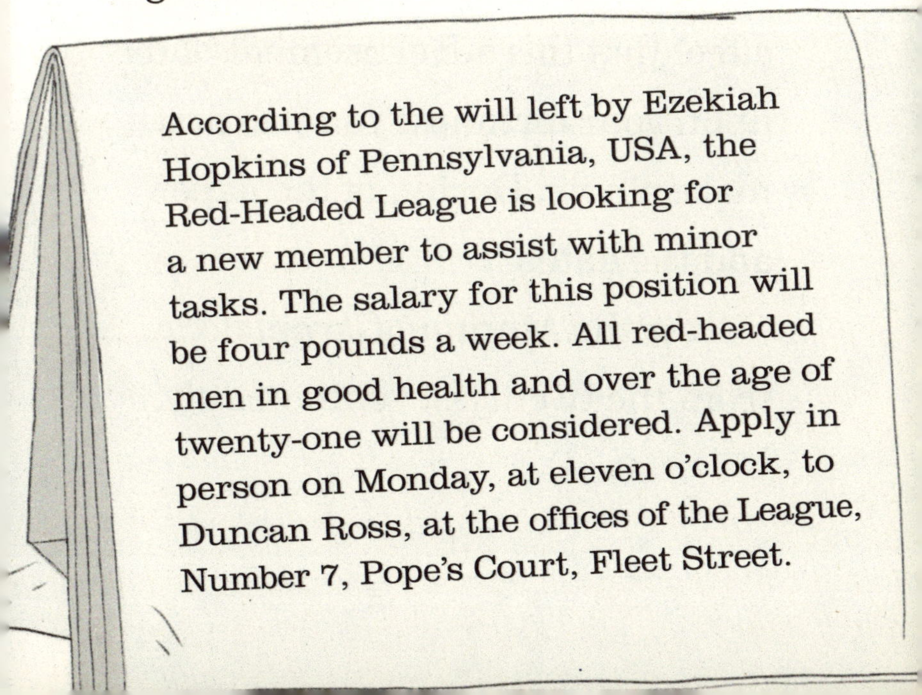

According to the will left by Ezekiah Hopkins of Pennsylvania, USA, the Red-Headed League is looking for a new member to assist with minor tasks. The salary for this position will be four pounds a week. All red-headed men in good health and over the age of twenty-one will be considered. Apply in person on Monday, at eleven o'clock, to Duncan Ross, at the offices of the League, Number 7, Pope's Court, Fleet Street.

'What on earth does this mean?' I cried after I had read the extraordinary advertisement twice.

Holmes chuckled and wriggled in his chair. 'It is a little off the beaten track, isn't it?' he said. 'And now, Mr Wilson, tell us about yourself, your household, and the effect that this advertisement had upon your fortunes. You will first make a note, Doctor, of the paper and the date.'

'It is the *Morning Chronicle*, from the twenty-seventh of July,

1890. Just two months ago.'

'Very good. Now, Mr Wilson?'

'Well, it is just as I have been telling you, Mr Sherlock Holmes,' said Jabez Wilson, mopping his forehead. 'I have a small pawnbroker's business in Saxe-Coburg Square, near the City. It's not a very large affair, and in recent years it has not done more than just give me a living. I used to be able

to keep two assistants, but now I only keep one. I would have a job to pay him, but he is willing to come for half wages so as to learn the business.'

'What is the name of this obliging youth?'

'His name is Vincent Spaulding and he's not such a youth either. It's hard to say his age. I should not wish for a smarter assistant, Mr Holmes, and I know very well that he could do better and earn twice what I am able to give him. But after all, he is satisfied, so why should I put ideas in his head?'

'Why indeed? You are fortunate in having an employee who comes under the full market price. It's not a common experience. Your assistant seems as remarkable as your advertisement.'

I had to agree. There couldn't be many employers who had the good fortune to take on an assistant willing to work for so little.

'Oh, he has his faults too,' said Mr Wilson. 'Never was such a fellow so keen on photography.

Snapping away with a camera when he should be improving his mind, and then diving down into the cellar like a rabbit into its hole to develop his pictures. That's his main fault. On the whole, he's a good worker. There's no vice in him.'

'He is still with you, I presume?'

'Yes, sir. He and a girl of fourteen, who does some simple cooking and keeps the place clean – that's all I have in the house, for I lost my wife many years ago and we never had any family. We live very quietly, sir, the three of us, and we keep a roof over our heads and pay our debts, if we do nothing more.'

'It was that advertisement that started this mess. Spaulding came down to the office just eight weeks ago to this day, with this very paper in his hand, and he says, "I wish to the Lord, Mr Wilson, that I was a red-headed man."

'"Why is that?" I asks.

'"Why," says he, "here's another vacancy in the League

of the Red-Headed Men. It's worth quite a little fortune to any man who gets it, and I hear that there are more jobs than men to fill them. If my hair would only change colour, here's a nice little job all ready for me to step into."'

Wilson looked at my companion earnestly. 'You see, Mr Holmes, I am a very stay-at-home man. I do not need to go looking for customers; they come to me. I run my business from my house, so you see there are often weeks on end when I don't step outside. I don't know much of what goes on, so was glad of some news. I asked my assistant what this League was.'

'"Have you never heard of the League of Red-Headed Men?" Spaulding asked me, and I said

I hadn't. He seemed shocked, but as I said, it is very easy for news to pass me by.

'"But you are suitable yourself for one of their vacancies," he said. I asked him what it was worth and he said a couple of hundred pounds a year, but the work was very simple and need not interfere with my other occupation. Well, that made me prick up my ears, for the extra couple of hundred pounds would have been very handy. Business has been very slow for several years now.'

With this, Mr Wilson broke off his narrative and glanced between Holmes and I, as if looking for agreement or sympathy.

Holmes nodded. 'Please continue.'

Our client coughed then furrowed his brow as he recalled the conversation. 'I asked him to tell me all about this league.

'"Well," said Spaulding, "as far as I can make out the League was founded by an American millionaire, Ezekiah Hopkins, who was very peculiar in his ways. He was himself red-headed, and he wished to give all red-headed men the same opportunities he had enjoyed. When he died, he left his enormous fortune in the hands of trustees, with instructions to use the money for the benefit of men whose hair was of that colour."

'"But," said I, "there would be millions of red-headed men who would apply."

'"Not so many as you might think," said Spaulding. "You see, the work is limited to Londoners, and to grown

men. Hopkins was actually born in London, and he wanted to repay the debt he felt he owed the town. Then again, I have heard that it is no use applying if your hair is anything but real bright, blazing, fiery red. If you cared to apply, Mr Wilson, you would just walk in, but perhaps it would hardly be worth your while for the sake of a few hundred pounds."'

Chapter Three

'Now, gentlemen,' said Wilson, 'you

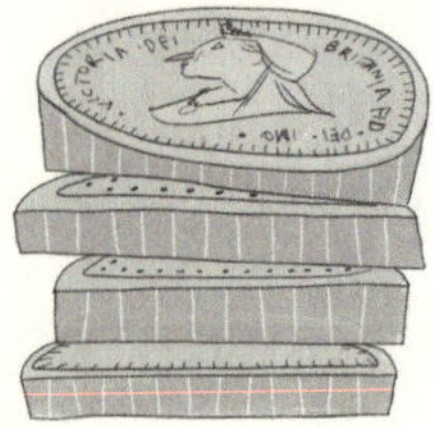

can see that my hair is the colour Spaulding described, so it seemed to me that I stood as good a chance as any man. Vincent Spaulding seemed to know so much about it that I thought he might prove useful, so I ordered him to put up the shutters for the day and to come right away with me. He was very willing to have a day's holiday so we started off for the address that was given in the advertisement.

'I never hope to see such a sight again, Mr Holmes. Every man who had a shade of red in his hair had answered the advertisement. I should not have thought there were so many in the whole country as were brought together by that single vacancy. When I saw how many were waiting I would have given up in despair, but Spaulding would not hear of it. How he did it I could not imagine, but he pushed and butted until he got me through the crowd and right up the steps that led to the office.

'There was a double stream upon the stairs – one of men going up in hope and the other made up of disappointed fellows who had been rejected. We soon found ourselves in the office.'

'Your story is certainly interesting so far,' Holmes said encouragingly, making some notes on his shirt cuff.

'There was nothing in the office but a couple of wooden chairs and a table, behind which sat a small man with a head that was even redder than mine. He said a few words to each candidate as they came up and then he always managed to find some fault that would disqualify them. Getting the job did not seem to be such an easy matter after all. However, when our turn came, the little man was friendlier to me than to any of the others. He even closed the door as we entered, so that he might have a private word with us.

'"This is Mr Jabez Wilson," said my assistant, "and he is willing to fill a vacancy in the League."

'"And he is well suited for it," the interviewer answered. "He has every requirement. I cannot recall when I have seen anything so fine." He took a step backwards, cocked his head on one side, and gazed at my hair until I felt quite embarrassed. Then, suddenly, he stepped forwards, shook my hand, and congratulated me warmly on my success.'

'"You will, I am sure, excuse me for taking an obvious precaution," he said. Then he seized my hair with both his hands and tugged until I yelled with pain. "We have to be careful, for we have twice been fooled by wigs and once by paint." Then he stepped over to the open window and shouted at the top of his voice that the vacancy had been filled. A groan of disappointment came up from below, and the folk all trooped away in different directions until there was not a red head to be seen except

my own and that of the manager.

'"My name," said he, "is Mr Duncan Ross, and I am one of the trustees of the fund set up by Ezekiah Hopkins. When shall you be able to begin your new duties?"

'"Well, it is a little awkward," I said, "for I have a business already."

'"Oh, never mind about that, Mr Wilson," said Vincent Spaulding. "I shall be able to look after that for you."

'"What would be the hours?" I asked.

'"Ten until two."

'Now, a pawnbroker's business

is mostly done in the evening, Mr Holmes, especially Thursday and Friday evening, which is just before pay day, so it would suit me very well to earn a little in the mornings. Besides, I knew that my assistant was a good man and that he would see to anything that needed doing. So I told him that those hours would suit me fine and asked about the pay.

'"Four pounds a week."

'"And the work?"

'"Is very easy. There is only one condition: you are absolutely forbidden to leave the building for any reason. If you leave, you forfeit your position forever. You will not meet the conditions if you budge from the office during that time."

"It's only four hours a day, and I should not think of leaving," I said.

"'No excuse will count," said Mr Duncan Ross, "neither sickness, nor business, nor anything else."

"'And the work?"

"'Is to copy out the *Encyclopaedia Britannica*. There is the first volume of it on that shelf. You must find your own ink, pens, and blotting paper, but

we provide this table and chair. Will you be ready tomorrow?"

'"Certainly," I answered.

'"Then goodbye, Mr Jabez Wilson, and let me congratulate you once more on the important position you have been fortunate enough to gain." He showed me out of the room, and I went home with my assistant. I hardly knew what to say or do, I was so pleased at my own good fortune.

'Well, I thought the matter over all day, and by the evening I was in low spirits again. I convinced myself that the whole affair must be some great hoax or fraud, though I could not imagine what the point of it was. It seemed altogether beyond belief that anyone could make such a will or that they would pay such a sum for doing anything so simple as copying out the *Encyclopaedia Britannica*. Vincent Spaulding did what he could to cheer me up, but by bedtime I had talked myself out of the whole thing.'

Chapter Four

Wilson paused again. I could well

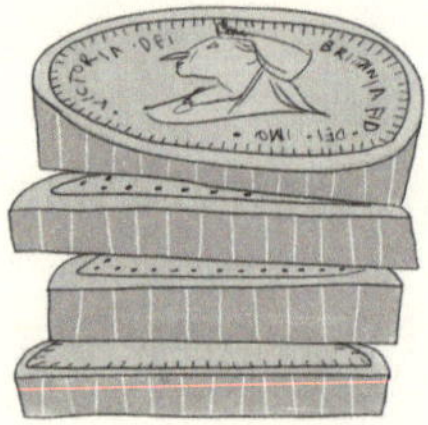

understand his doubts. The whole thing seemed to have no purpose at all. I glanced at Holmes, but I could not read his expression. He had remained very still throughout the story and, although he seemed far away in thought, I knew that he was listening intently.

Mr Wilson continued. 'In the morning I determined to have a look at it anyhow, so I bought a penny bottle of ink, a small quill pen and seven sheets of paper. Then I started off for Pope's Court.

'Well, to my surprise and delight, everything was as right as possible. The table was set out ready for me and Mr Duncan Ross was there to see that I got to work. He started me off upon the letter A and then he left me, but he would drop in from time to time to see that all was right with me. At two

o'clock he wished me good day, complimented me on the amount that I had written, and locked the door of the office after me.

'This went on day after day, Mr Holmes, and on Saturday the manager came in and plonked down four golden sovereigns for my week's work. It was the same the next week and the week after. Every morning I was there at ten, and every afternoon I left at two. Gradually, Mr Duncan Ross took to coming in only once in the morning and then, after a time, he did not come in at all. Still, of course, I never dared to leave the room for an instant, for I was not sure when he might come, and the job was such a good one, and suited me so well, that I could not risk the loss of it.

'Eight weeks passed like this and I had written about Abbots and Archery, and Armour and Architecture, and Attica, and I hoped that I might get on to the B's before very long. It cost me something in paper and I had pretty near filled a shelf with my writings. Then, suddenly, the whole thing came to an end.'

'To an end?'

'Yes, sir. And just this morning. I went to my work as usual at ten o'clock, but the door was shut and locked, with a little square of cardboard tacked on it. Here it is, and you can read it for yourself.'

He held up a piece of white cardboard.

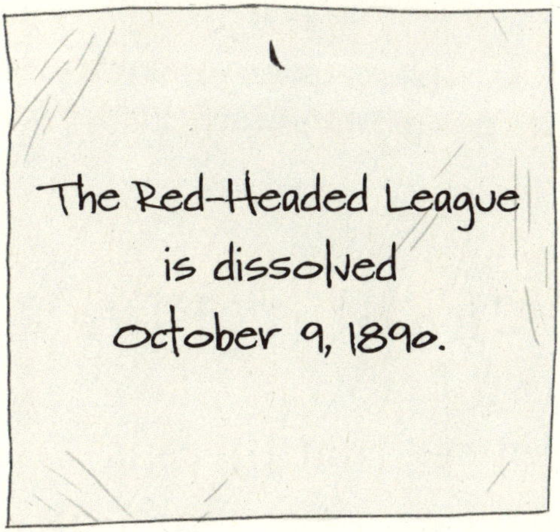

Holmes and I looked at the curt note and the sorry face behind it, and we both burst into a roar of laughter.

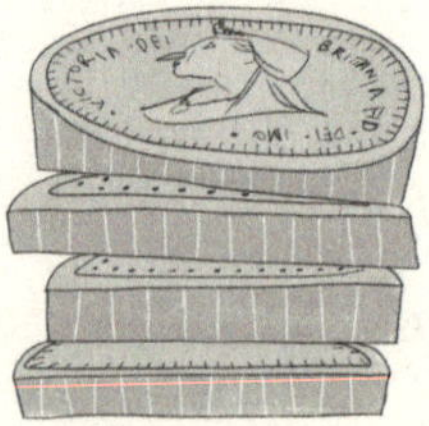

Chapter Five

'I cannot see that there is anything funny,' said our client, his face going as red as his hair. 'If you can do nothing but laugh at me then I'll go elsewhere.'

'No, no,' cried Holmes, pushing him back into the chair from which he'd half risen. 'I really wouldn't miss your case for the world. It is most refreshingly unusual. But there is, if you will excuse me, something just a little funny about it. What did you do when you found the notice on the door?'

'I was staggered, sir. I did not know what to do. I called at the offices nearby but no one knew anything about it. Finally, I went to the landlord, who lives on the

'"What, the red-headed man?" he asked. "His name was William Morris. He was a solicitor, and was using the room temporarily until his new premises were ready. He moved out yesterday."

'I asked if he knew where I could find him.

'"At his new offices: Number 17, King Edward Street, near St Paul's," he told me.

'I went there, Mr Holmes, but it was a factory that made artificial kneecaps and no one had ever heard of either Mr William Morris or Mr Duncan Ross.'

The idea of this almost made me chuckle again, but I stopped myself just in time.

'And what did you do then?' asked Holmes, struggling to keep a straight face himself.

'I went home to Saxe-Coburg Square and asked the advice of my assistant, but he could not help in any way.

He suggested that I wait to hear by post, but that was not good enough, Mr Holmes. I did not wish to lose such a job without a struggle so, as I had heard that you were good enough to give advice to poor folk who were in need of it, I came right away to you.'

'And you did very wisely,' said Holmes. 'Your case is a very remarkable one, and I shall be happy to look into it. From what you have told me, I think this is more serious than it might appear.'

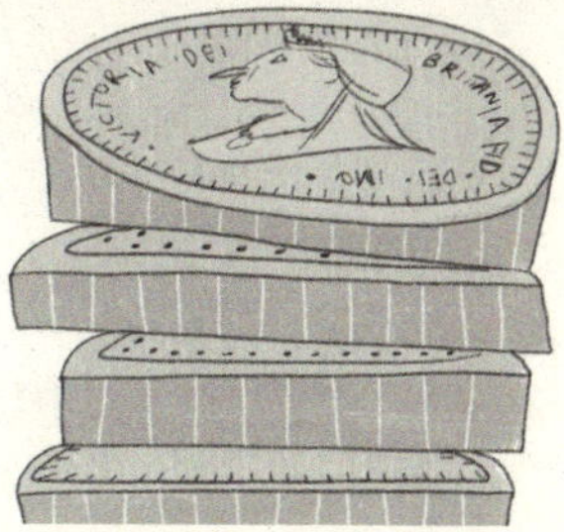

‘Serious enough,’ he said, ‘for I have lost four pounds a week.’

‘I do not see that you have any complaints against this league,’ said Holmes. ‘You are richer by some thirty pounds, to say nothing of the knowledge you have gained on every subject under the letter A. You have lost nothing by them.’

‘No, sir, but I want to find out about them. Who they are, and what their reason was in playing such a prank, if that’s what it was.

It was a pretty expensive joke for them.'

'We shall try to clear up these points for you. First, one or two questions, Mr Wilson. How long has this assistant of yours been with you?'

'He had been working for me about a month when I took up the job with the League.'

'How did he come?'

'In answer to an advertisement.'

'Was he the only applicant?'

'No, I had a dozen.'

'Why did you pick him?'

'Because he was handy and would come cheap.'

'At half wages, in fact.'

'Yes.'

'What is he like, this Vincent Spaulding?'

'Small, stoutly built, very quick in his ways, and no hair on his face though he's over thirty. He has a white acid splash on his forehead.'

Holmes sat up in his chair in excitement. 'I thought as much,' he said. 'Have you ever noticed that his ears are pierced for earrings?'

'Yes, sir. He told me that it had been done when he was a lad.'

'Hmm,' said Holmes, sinking back deep in thought. 'He is still with you?'

'Oh, yes, sir.'

'And he is taking care of your business while you are away?'

'Yes. I have no reason to complain about him looking after

things. There's never very much to do in the mornings.'

'I think we have heard all we need,' my friend replied. 'Thank you. I shall be happy to give you an opinion on the subject in a day or two, Mr Wilson. Today is Saturday, and I hope that by Monday we may come to a conclusion.'

'Well, Watson,' said Holmes, when our visitor had left us. 'What do you make of it all?'

'I make nothing of it,' I answered truthfully. 'It is a most mysterious business.'

'As a rule,' said Holmes, 'the more bizarre a thing is, the less mysterious it proves to be. It is the ordinary crimes that are really puzzling.'

I had heard him say this before, but it didn't help my own reasoning. 'What are you going to do then?'

'I need to consider the matter. I beg that you won't speak to me for fifty minutes.'

He curled himself up in his chair with his thin knees drawn up under his hawk-like nose, and there he sat with his eyes closed and his black clay pipe thrusting out like the bill of some strange bird.

I thought he had fallen asleep and was indeed nodding off myself, when he suddenly sprang out of his chair like a man who had made up his mind, and put his pipe down on the mantelpiece.

'The violinist, Sarasate, is playing at St James' Hall this afternoon,' he said. 'Could your patients spare you for a few hours?'

'I have nothing to do today.'

'Then put on your hat and come. I am going through the City first, and we can have some lunch on the way. I believe that there is a good deal of German music on the programme, which is rather more to my taste than Italian or French. Come along!'

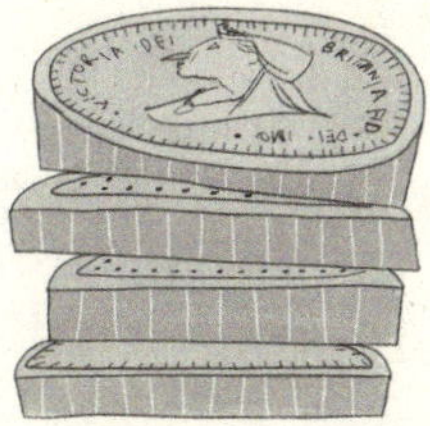

Chapter Six

I was glad of the prospect of a pleasant afternoon and surprised that Holmes should ask me to accompany him. He often preferred his own company.

We travelled by Underground as far as Aldersgate and a short walk took us to Saxe-Coburg Square, the scene of the strange story that we had listened to that morning.

It was a shabby place, where

four lines of miserable, two-storied brick houses looked out over a small square containing a lawn of weedy grass and a few clumps of faded laurel bushes. On the corner building, a brown board with *Jabez Wilson* in white letters showed the place where our red-headed client carried on his business. Holmes stopped in front of it with his head on one side and looked it all over, his eyes shining brightly. Then he walked slowly up the street and then down again to the corner, still looking at the houses. Next, he returned to the pawnbroker's and thumped vigorously on the pavement with his stick two or three times, much to my confusion. Finally Holmes went up to the door and knocked. It was instantly opened by a bright-looking, clean-shaven young fellow, who asked him to step in.

'Thank you,' said Holmes. 'I only wished to ask you how you would go from here to the Strand.'

'Third right, fourth left,' answered the assistant promptly, closing the door.

'Smart fellow, that,' observed Holmes as we walked away.

'You clearly believe that Mr Wilson's assistant is an important part of this mystery. I am sure that you asked for directions just to see him.'

'Not him.'

'What then?'

'The knees of his trousers.'

'And what did you see?'

'What I expected to see.'

'Why did you tap your stick on the pavement?'

'My dear Doctor, this is a time for observation, not for talk. We are spies in an enemy's country. We know something of Saxe-Coburg Square. Let us now explore the area around it.'

I thought that I could have observed better had I known what I was looking for, but I knew better than to argue with

Holmes at a time like this.

We turned the corner and found ourselves on a very different road. It was one of the main roads taking the traffic of the City to the north and west. The road was blocked by a huge stream of vehicles flowing into

and out of central London, while the footpaths were black with the swarm of pedestrians. It was hard to believe that the fine shops and businesses lining this street connected it with the drab and rundown square we had just left.

'Let me see,' said Holmes, standing on the corner. 'I should just like to remember the order of the houses just here. It is a hobby of mine to have an exact knowledge of London. There is Mortimer's, the tobacconist, the little newspaper shop, the Coburg branch of the City and Suburban Bank, the Vegetarian Restaurant, and McFarlane's carriage-builders.

'And now, Doctor, we've done our work, so it's time for some play. A sandwich and a cup of coffee and then we're off to violin land, where all is sweetness and harmony, and there are no red-headed clients to annoy us with their puzzles.'

My friend was not only an enthusiastic and talented violinist but a composer too. All afternoon he sat in the stalls completely happy, gently waving his long thin fingers in time to the music. His gently smiling face and dreamy eyes were very different from those of Holmes the keen-witted criminal agent. I marvelled at how he could take such pleasure in idleness yet be so exact and motivated at the same time, but it occurred to me that these were two sides of the same coin. Holmes' passion for music was only matched by his passion for his work; his absorption in one was often countered by enthusiasm in

the other. When I saw him that afternoon so engaged in the music at St James' Hall, I felt that an evil time might be coming upon those whom he had set himself to hunt down.

'You want to go home, no doubt, Doctor?' he said as we emerged from the concert hall.

'Yes, it would be as well.'

'And I have some business to do that will take some hours. This business at Saxe-Coburg Square is serious.'

'Why serious?'

'A considerable crime is being planned. I have every reason to believe that we shall be in time to stop it, but today being Saturday rather complicates matters. I shall want your help tonight.'

'At what time?'

'Ten will be early enough.'

'I shall be at Baker Street at ten.'

'Very well, Doctor. ' Holmes waved his hand, turned on his heel, and disappeared in an instant among the crowd.

I didn't think that I was denser than the average

person, but I always felt a little foolish when I was with Sherlock Holmes. I had heard what he had heard, I had seen what he had seen, and yet from his words it was evident that he understood clearly not only what had happened, but what was about to happen. Meanwhile I still couldn't make any sense of this puzzle.

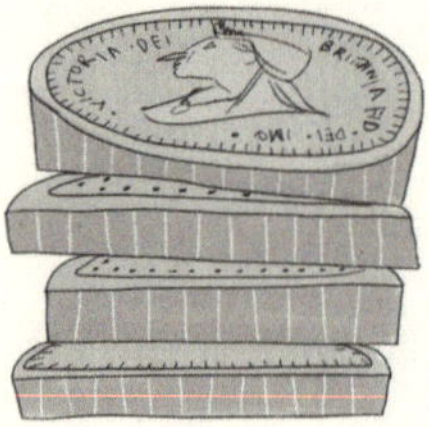

Chapter Seven

As I drove home to my house in Kensington I thought over it all, from the extraordinary story of the red-headed copier of the *Encyclopaedia Britannica* down to the visit in Saxe-Coburg Square, and the ominous words with which Holmes had departed. What was this nocturnal expedition? Where were we going and what were we to do? I had the hint from Holmes that the smooth-faced pawnbroker's assistant was a formidable man who might play a cunning game. I tried to puzzle it out, but gave up in despair and put it out of my mind until the night should bring an explanation.

It was quarter past nine when I started from home and made my way across Hyde Park and so through Oxford Street to Baker Street. Two hansom cabs were standing at the door and, as I entered the hallway, I heard the sound of voices from above.

On entering Holmes' room, I found him in animated conversation with two men, one of whom I recognised as Athelney Jones, a Scotland Yard detective. The other was a long, thin, sad-faced man, with a very shiny top hat and respectable frock-coat.

'Ha! Our party is complete,' said Holmes, buttoning up his jacket and taking his heavy hunting crop from the rack. 'Watson, you

Hunting crop

My weapon of choice. Light and portable. Useful because of speed. Easily goes unnoticed. The loaded crop is most effective – same design but has a shaft filled with lead. The original use for crops is to control a horse, along with voice, legs and position in saddle.

know Mr Jones, of Scotland Yard. Let me introduce you to Mr Merryweather, who is to be our companion in tonight's adventure.'

'We're hunting in pairs again, Doctor, you see,' said Jones. 'Our friend Holmes is a wonderful man for starting a chase. All he wants is

an old dog to help him to do the running down.'

'I hope a wild goose may not be at the end of our chase,' observed Mr Merryweather, gloomily.

'You may have great confidence in Mr Holmes, sir,' said Jones, loftily. 'He has his own little methods which are, if he won't mind me saying so, just a little too fantastic, but he has the makings of a detective in him. Once or twice, as in the business of the Sholto murder and the Agra treasure, he has been more nearly correct than the official force.'

'Oh, if you say so, Mr Jones,' said the stranger, with respect. 'Still, I confess that I miss my game of bridge. It is the first Saturday night for thirty-seven years that I have not had my game.'

'I think you will find,' said Holmes, 'that you will play for a higher stake tonight than you have ever done yet, and the game will be more exciting. For you, Mr Merryweather, the stake will be some thirty thousand pounds and for you, Jones, it will be the man upon whom you wish to lay your hands.'

'John Clay, the murderer, thief and forger,' said Jones.

'He's a young man, Mr Merryweather, but he's at the top of his profession and I would rather have my handcuffs on him than any criminal in London.

'He's a remarkable man, is young John Clay. His grandfather was a royal duke and he himself has been to Eton and Oxford.

His brain is as cunning as his fingers, and although we meet signs of him at every turn, we never know where to find the man himself. He'll be doing a robbery in Scotland one week and raising money to build an orphanage in Cornwall the next. I've been on his track for years and have never set eyes on him yet.'

'I hope that I may have the pleasure of introducing you tonight,' said Holmes. 'I've also had one or two little run-ins with Mr John Clay. It is past ten, however, and quite time that we started out. If you two will take the first hansom cab, Watson and I will follow in the second.'

Holmes didn't speak during the long drive and lay back humming the tunes that he had heard in the afternoon. We rattled through the endless maze of gas-lit streets until we emerged into Farringdon Street.

'We are close now,' my friend remarked. 'This fellow, Merryweather, is a

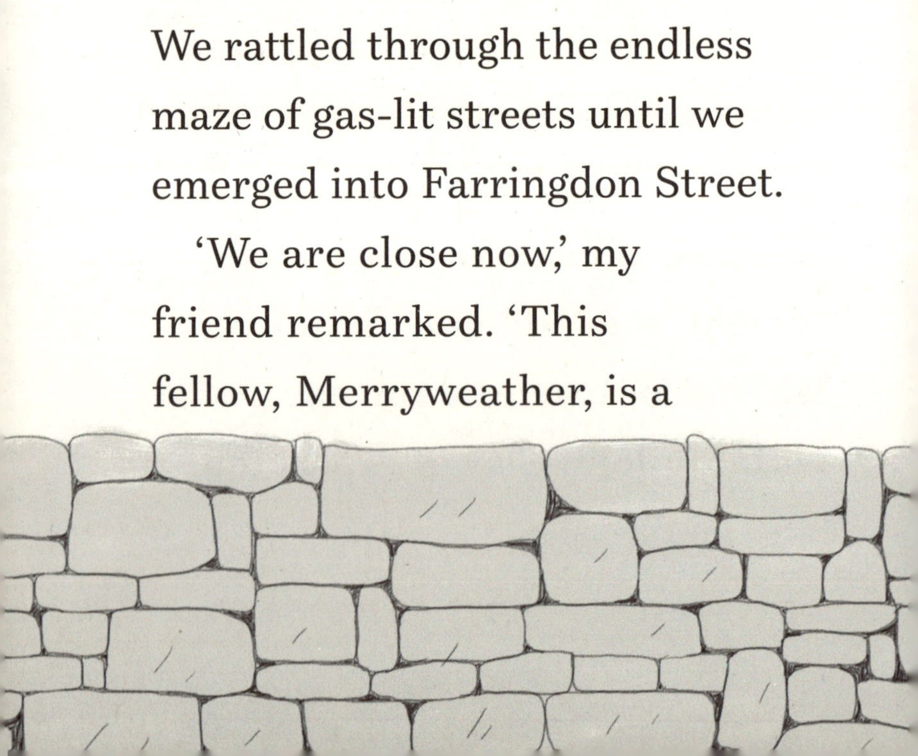

bank director and personally interested in the matter. I thought it was as well to have Jones with us as well. I suppose he is not a bad fellow, though an absolute idiot in his profession, as I'm sure you remember. He has one positive virtue, though. He is as brave as a bulldog and as tenacious as a lobster if he gets his claws into anyone. Here we are, and they are waiting for us.'

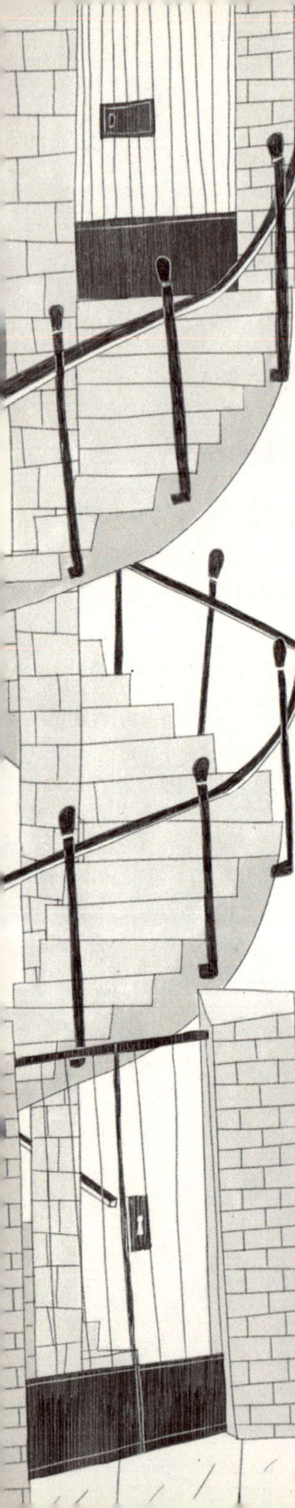

We had reached the same crowded street where we had been in the morning. Our cabs were dismissed and, following Mr Merryweather, we went down a narrow passage and through a side door. Inside, there was a small corridor,

which ended in a massive iron gate. This led down a flight of winding stone steps, which ended in another big gate. Mr Merryweather stopped to light a lantern and then led us down a dark, earth-smelling passage and, after opening a third door, into a huge vault.

'No one could access this room from above,' Holmes remarked as he held up the lantern and gazed

at the crates and massive boxes piled around the room.

'Nor from below,' said Mr Merryweather, striking his stick on the paving stones that lined the floor. He looked up in surprise. 'Why, dear me, it sounds quite hollow!'

'I really must ask you to be a little more quiet,' said Holmes, severely. 'You have already endangered the whole success of our expedition. Might I ask that you sit down upon one of those boxes and not interfere?'

The solemn Mr Merryweather perched himself on a crate with a very injured expression on his face while Holmes fell on his knees on the floor and, with the lantern and magnifying glass, began to examine minutely the cracks between the stones.

After a few seconds he sprang to his feet again and put the magnifying glass in his pocket.

'We have at least an hour to wait,' he said. 'They can hardly do anything until the good pawnbroker is in bed. Then they will not lose a minute, for the sooner they do their work, the more time they will have for their escape.'

Holmes looked at me. 'Doctor, you will no doubt have realised that we are in the cellar of the City branch of one of the principal London banks. Mr Merryweather is their chairman of directors, and he will explain to you that there are reasons why the more daring criminals of London should take a great interest in this cellar at present.'

'It is our French gold,' added the director. 'We have had several warnings that an attempt might be made to steal it.'

'Your French gold?'

'Yes. Some months ago we needed to strengthen our

resources and borrowed thirty thousand Napoleon gold coins from the Bank of France. It has become known that we never needed to unpack the money and that it is still lying in our cellar. The crate upon which I sit contains two thousand Napoleon coins packed between layers of lead foil. Our gold reserve is much more than we would normally keep in one branch, and the directors were worried about it.'

'And rightly so,' said Holmes. 'But now is the time that we

arranged our little plans. I expect that within an hour things will come to a head. In the meantime, Mr Merryweather, we must put the screen over that lantern.'

'And sit in the dark?'

'I'm afraid so. I thought of bringing some cards so you could have your game after all, but I see that the enemy's preparation has gone so far that we cannot risk showing a light.

'First of all,' Holmes continued, 'we must choose our positions. These are daring men and, although we shall take them by surprise, they may do us some harm unless we are careful. I shall stand behind this crate, and you hide yourself behind those. Then, when I flash a light upon them, close in quickly.'

Holmes pushed the slide across the lantern, and left us in pitch darkness – darker than I've ever experienced before. The smell of hot metal remained to assure us that the light was still there, ready to flash out at a moment's notice. There was something depressing about the sudden gloom in the cold, dank air of the vault.

'They have only one escape route,' whispered Holmes. 'That is back through the house into Saxe-Coburg Square. I hope that you have done what I asked you, Jones?'

'I have an inspector and two officers waiting at the front door.'

'Then we have blocked all the holes. And now we must be silent and wait.'

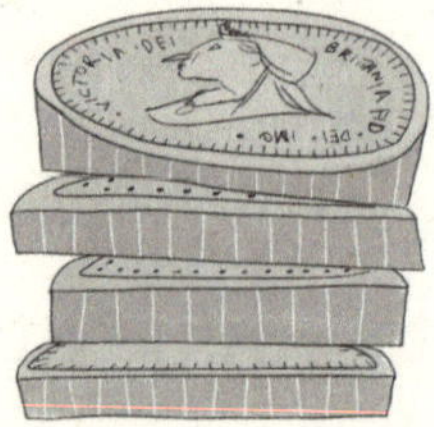

Chapter Eight

What a time it seemed! It was actually only an hour and a quarter, yet it seemed to me that it was most of the night. My limbs were tired and still, for I was afraid to move and make a noise. My nerves were frayed, and my hearing was so acute that I could hear the breathing of my companions. I passed the time by learning to distinguish between the deeper, heavier breathing of

Jones and the thin sighing note of the bank director.

Suddenly my eyes caught the glint of a light.

At first it was a faint spark on the stone paving. Then it lengthened out until it became a yellow line, and then, without any warning or sound, it expanded and seemed to open. A hand appeared.

This delicate white hand felt about in the centre of the little area of light for a minute or more. Then it was suddenly withdrawn and all was dark again except for the single spark, which marked a chink between the stones.

The hand disappeared for only a moment. Then, with a rending, tearing sound, one of the broad, white stones turned over on its side and left a square, gaping hole through which streamed the light of a lantern. A clean-cut, boyish face peeped out over the edge.

He looked about and then, with a hand on either side of the hole, drew himself shoulder high and waist high until one knee rested on the edge. In another instant he stood at the side of the hole and was hauling a companion after him; one as lithe and small as himself, with a pale face and a shock of very red hair.

'It's all clear,' he whispered. 'Have you the chisel and the bags? – Great Scott! Jump, Archie!'

Sherlock Holmes had sprung up and seized the intruder by the collar. The other dived down the hole and I heard the sound of ripping cloth as Jones clutched at his clothes. The light flashed on the barrel of a revolver, but Holmes' hunting crop came down on the man's wrist, and the gun clinked upon the stone floor.

'It's no use, John Clay,' said Holmes. 'You have no chance at all.'

'So I see,' the other answered with utmost coolness. 'I think my pal is all right, although I see that you have his coat-tails.'

'There are three men waiting for him at the door,' said Holmes.

'Oh, indeed. You seem to have done the thing very completely. I must compliment you.'

'And I you,' Holmes answered. 'Your red-headed idea was very new and effective.'

I looked at Jones and Mr Merryweather to see if they were as confused as I was by the

tone of the conversation between Holmes and Clay.

While the bank manager and I looked on, Jones was fumbling with a pair of handcuffs. 'You'll see your pal again soon,' he said to Clay. 'He's quicker at climbing down holes than I am. Just hold out your hands while I fix these handcuffs.'

'I beg that you will not touch me with your filthy hands,' said our prisoner as the cuffs clattered upon his wrists. 'You may not be aware that I have royal blood in my veins. Have the goodness when you address me to say "sir" and "please".'

'All right,' said Jones, with a stare and a snigger. 'Well, would you please, sir, march upstairs where we can get a cab to carry your highness to the police station.'

'That's better,' said John Clay serenely. He made a sweeping bow to the three of us, and walked quietly off in the custody of the detective. The sudden relief that it was all over made me appreciate Jones' sarcasm, and I smiled.

'Really, Mr Holmes,' said Mr Merryweather as we followed them from the cellar. 'I do not know how the bank can thank you or repay you. There's no doubt that you have detected and defeated one of the most determined attempts at bank robbery that I have ever seen.'

'I have had one or two little scores of my own to settle with Mr John Clay,' said Holmes. 'I have had a little expense in my investigation, which I shall expect the bank to repay, but beyond that I am repaid. I have had an experience that is in many ways unique, and I have heard the very remarkable story of the Red-Headed League.'

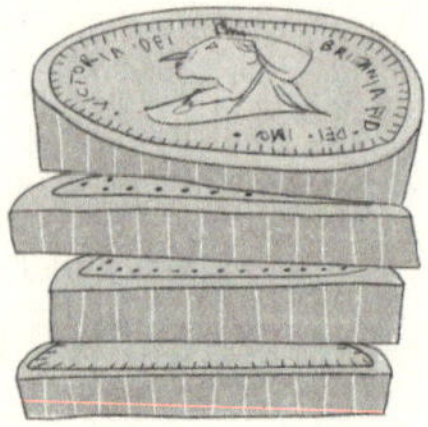

Chapter Nine

'You see, Watson,' Holmes explained in the early hours of the morning as we sat over our cups of tea in Baker Street, 'it was perfectly obvious to me that the advertisement and the task

of copying out the *Encyclopaedia Britannica* were designed to get Mr Wilson out of the way for a few hours every day. It was a curious way of managing it, but it would be difficult to suggest a better one. Clay was probably given the idea by the colour of his accomplice's hair. The four pounds a week was a lure that would attract their target, and what was that to them? They were playing for thousands!'

I thought I detected a hint of respect in Holmes' voice. So that was why he had been so pleasant to Clay during his capture! In the same way that Holmes was not afraid to express criticism, he would always acknowledge others' brilliance. Even I had to admit that Clay's plan was particularly clever.

Holmes continued. 'They put in the advertisement. One rogue has the temporary office, the other encourages Mr Wilson to apply for it, and together they make sure of his absence every morning during the week. From the time I heard of the assistant having come for half wages, it was obvious to me that he had some strong motive for getting the job.'

'But how could you guess what the motive was?'

'Mr Wilson's business was a small one and there was nothing in his house that could account for such elaborate preparations and such a cost. It must then be something out of the house. What could it be? I thought of the assistant's fondness for photography and his habit of vanishing into the cellar. He was doing something there that took many hours a day for months on end. I could think of nothing except that he must be tunnelling to some other building.'

I nodded. It was all perfectly logical, looking back.

'When we went to visit the scene of the action, I surprised you by beating on the pavement with my stick to see whether the

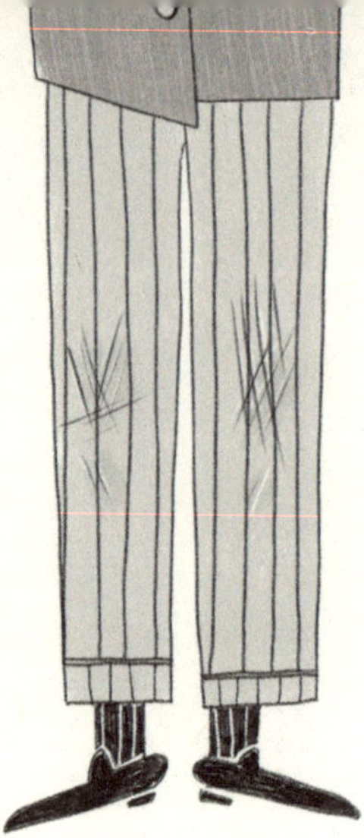

cellar stretched out in front or behind. It was not in front. Then I rang the bell and, as I hoped, the assistant opened it. We have had some skirmishes, but we had never set eyes on each other before. I hardly looked at his face. His knees were what I wished to see. You must have noticed how worn, wrinkled and stained they were. They were proof of long hours of burrowing. The only remaining point was what they were burrowing for.

I walked around the corner, saw the City and Suburban Bank joined onto our friend's premises, and felt that I had solved my problem. When you drove home after the concert, I called upon Scotland Yard and upon the chairman of the bank directors, with the result that you have seen.'

'And how could you tell that they would make their attempt tonight?'

'Well, when they closed their League offices, that was a sign that they no longer cared about Mr Jabez Wilson's presence at the pawnbroker's. In other words, they had completed their tunnel. It was essential, though, that they should use it soon as it might be discovered, or the gold might be moved.'

'And Saturday would suit them more than any other day,' I said, 'as it would give them two days to carry out the robbery and escape.'

'Precisely,' said Holmes. 'For all these reasons I expected them to come tonight.'

'I cannot find a single flaw in your reasoning,' I exclaimed in admiration. 'It is so long a chain, and yet every link rings true.'

'It saved me from boredom,' he answered, yawning. 'Alas! I already feel it closing in upon me. My life is spent in one long effort to escape from the ordinariness of life. These little problems help me to do so.'

'And in so doing, you help others with their problems.'

He shrugged his shoulders. 'Well, perhaps after all, I am of some little use.'

ENCYCLOPÆDIA
BRITANNICA

Sherlock Holmes

World-renowned private detective Sherlock Holmes has solved hundreds of mysteries, and is the author of such fascinating monographs as *Early English Charters* and *The Influence of a Trade Upon the Form of a Hand.* He keeps bees in his free time.

Dr John Watson

Wounded in action at Maiwand, Dr John Watson left the army and moved into 221B Baker Street. There he was surprised to learn that his new friend, Sherlock Holmes, faced daily peril solving crimes, and began documenting his investigations. Dr Watson also runs a doctor's practice.